Bicycles

by Lola M. Schaefer

Consultant:
Annette Thompson, Curator
The Bicycle Museum of America
New Bremen, Ohio

Bridgestone Books
an imprint of Capstone Press
Mankato, Minnesota

Bridgestone Books are published by Capstone Press
818 North Willow Street, Mankato, Minnesota 56001
http://www.capstone-press.com

Library of Congress Cataloging-in-Publication Data
Schaefer, Lola M., 1950–
Bicycles/by Lola M. Schaefer.
   p. cm.—(The transportation library)
   Includes bibliographical references and index.
   Summary: An introduction to bicycles, describing the main parts, how they work,
who invented them, how they are used as transportation, and more.
   ISBN 0-7368-0359-9
   1. Bicycles—Juvenile literature. [1. Bicycles and bicycling.] I. Title. II. Series.
TL412.S33   2000
629.227'2—dc21   99-13169
                                                                                           CIP

Editorial Credits
Mari C. Schuh and Blanche R. Bolland, editors; Timothy Halldin, cover designer
   and illustrator; Heather Kindseth, illustrator; Kimberly Danger, photo researcher

Photo Credits
The Bicycle Museum of America, New Bremen, Ohio, 14
Corbis, 16
FPG International LLC, 12
Gregg R. Andersen, cover
Karuna Eberl, 8
Photophile/Jeff Greenberg, 18
Transparencies, Inc./Michael Moore, 4
Unicorn Stock Photos/Wayne Floyd, 6
Visuals Unlimited/Mark E. Gibson, 20

Table of Contents

Bicycles

A bicycle is a vehicle with two wheels. A rider pedals to move a bicycle. A rider moves handlebars to steer. People ride bicycles short distances and long distances. Bicycles move faster than people can walk.

vehicle
something that carries people from one place to another

Traveling by Bicycle

Many people ride bicycles every day. Some children travel to school on bicycles. Some adults ride bicycles to work. Bicycle riders travel on streets and on bicycle paths. To stay safe, riders wear helmets and obey traffic rules.

traffic

moving cars and other types of vehicles on roads

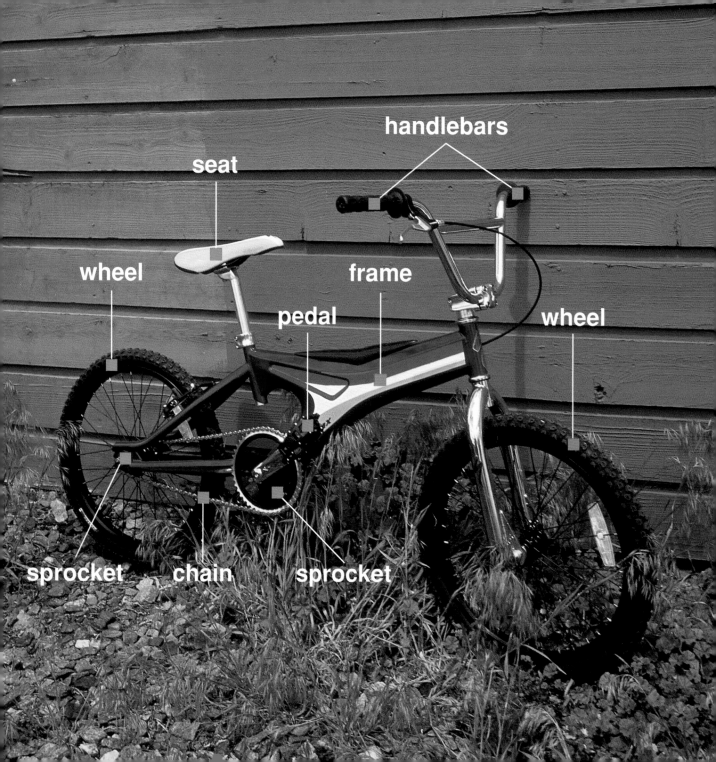

handlebars

seat

wheel

frame

pedal

wheel

sprocket

chain

sprocket

Parts of a Bicycle

All bicycles have the same main parts. A bicycle has two wheels, two pedals, two sprockets, and two brakes. A chain connects the sprockets. A bicycle has a metal frame. A seat is on the back of the frame. Handlebars are on the front of the frame.

sprocket
a wheel with a rim of toothlike points that fit into the holes of a chain

back wheel

front wheel

pedal

back sprocket

chain

pedal

front sprocket

How a Bicycle Works

Riders make bicycles move. Riders use their feet to push bicycle pedals in circles. The pedals turn the front sprocket. This sprocket moves the chain forward. The chain turns the back sprocket. The back wheel turns and makes the front wheel turn.

Before the Bicycle

People had three ways to travel on land before bicycles were invented. People walked. They rode horses. Or they rode in horse-drawn carriages or wagons. Bicycling was faster than walking. Bicycles needed less care than horses.

carriage
a vehicle with wheels that is usually pulled by horses

The Inventor of the Bicycle

In 1816, Baron Karl von Drais of Germany invented the first bicycle. He made his bicycle from wood. It did not have pedals. Karl pushed off the ground with his feet to move the bicycle forward. He steered with the bicycle's front handle.

Early Bicycles

Early bicycles were hard to ride. Their wood and iron wheels made rides bumpy on rough roads. Some bicycles were tall. The front wheel was larger than the back wheel. In 1885, James Starley made the first safety bicycle. This bicycle's rubber wheels were the same size.

Bicycles around the World

People around the world use bicycles. In China and Japan, bicycle riders fill the streets. Bicycles are more common than cars in these countries. Some countries have bicycle taxis. Riders pull passengers in carts behind bicycles.

Bicycle Facts

- Tandem bicycles carry two or more people.

- The average speed of a bicycle is 10 to 14 miles (16 to 23 kilometers) per hour.

- The fastest recorded speed of a bicycle is 166 miles (267 kilometers) per hour.

- Shanghai, China, is considered the bicycling center of the world. More than 2.5 million bicycle trips take place there every day.

- Brakes on the handlebars move a brake shoe to slow or stop the bicycle. The brake shoe presses against the rim of the wheel.

- A bicycle helmet protects a bicycle rider's head in an accident. Reflectors and lights help people see bicycles in the dark.

Hands On: How Sprockets Work

A rider pushes the pedals of a bicycle. The pedals move the sprockets. The sprockets move the wheels. You can see how sprockets make bicycling easier.

What You Need

A bicycle
A permanent marker
An adult

What You Do

1. With an adult, carefully turn the bicycle upside down so that it rests on the handlebars. The wheels will be in the air.
2. The adult should hold the bicycle in this position.
3. Mark the side of the back tire where it lines up with the bicycle frame.
4. Now place your hand on one pedal. Do not touch the tires or spokes.
5. Slowly push the pedal around for one complete turn.
6. At the same time, count how many times the mark on the back tire passes the bicycle frame.

Pushing the pedal around one complete turn can make the wheel turn many times. Sprockets help your bicycle move faster.

Words to Know

chain (CHAYN)—a series of metal rings joined together

helmet (HEL-mit)—a hard hat that protects the head

pedal (PED-uhl)—a lever on a bicycle that riders push with their feet

reflector (ri-FLEK-tur)—something shiny that bounces back light

steer (STEER)—to guide or direct

tandem (TAN-duhm)—a bicycle for two or more people that has one seat behind another

Read More

Coulter, George and Shirley Coulter. *Bicycles.* You Make It Work. Vero Beach, Fla.: Rourke, 1996.

Gibbons, Gail. *Bicycle Book.* New York: Holiday House, 1995.

Otfinoski, Steven. *Pedaling Along: Bikes Then and Now.* Here We Go! Tarrytown, N.Y.: Benchmark Books, 1997.

Raatma, Lucia. *Safety on Your Bicycle.* Safety First! Mankato, Minn.: Bridgestone Books, 1999.

Internet Sites

The Bicycle Museum of America
http://www.bicyclemuseum.com/html/bikes.html
Safety City Bike Tour
http://www.nhtsa.dot.gov/kids/biketour/index.html

Index

7/00

DATE DUE

AUG 1 5 2000	
OCT 1 2 2000	
OCT 0 6 2000	
NOV 0 4 2000	
NOV 2 9 2000	
MAR 2 8 2001	
MAR 2 9 2001	
APR 0 5 2001	
AUG 1 2 2002	
OCT 3 1 2002	
5/16/13	

BRODART, CO.   Cat. No. 23-221-003